W9-BMI-603

HOCUS POCUS

TO THOMAS, WHO DOES NOT NEED WORDS TO UNDERSTAND, AND TO ANDRÉ, WHO ALWAYS FINDS THE RIGHT ONES – S.D.

TO HARRY AND ANATOLE! – R.S.

Kids Can Press acknowledges the financial support of the Government of Ontario, through the Ontario Media Development Corporation's Ontario Book Initiative; the Ontario Arts Council; the Canada Council for the Arts; and the Government of Canada, through the BPIDP, for our publishing activity.

Published in Canada by
Kids Can Press Ltd.
25 Dockside Drive
Toronto, ON M5A 0B5

Published in the U.S. by
Kids Can Press Ltd.
2250 Military Road
Tonawanda, NY 14150

www.kidscanpress.com

The artwork in this book was rendered in Adobe Illustrator.

Edited by Tara Walker and Samantha Swenson
Designed by Marie Bartholomew

This book is smyth sewn casebound.
Manufactured in Shenzhen, China, in 4/2011 through Asia Pacific Offset

CM 11 0 9 8 7 6 5 4 3 2 1

Library and Archives Canada Cataloguing in Publication

Simard, Rémy
     Hocus pocus / Rémy Simard and Sylvie Desrosiers.

ISBN 978-1-55453-577-4

I. Desrosiers, Sylvie, 1954 - II. Title.

PS8587.I3065H63 2011   jC813'.54   C2011-900365-1

Kids Can Press is a CORUS™ Entertainment company

HOCUS POCUS

SYLVIE DESROSIERS

☆

RÉMY SIMARD

KIDS CAN PRESS

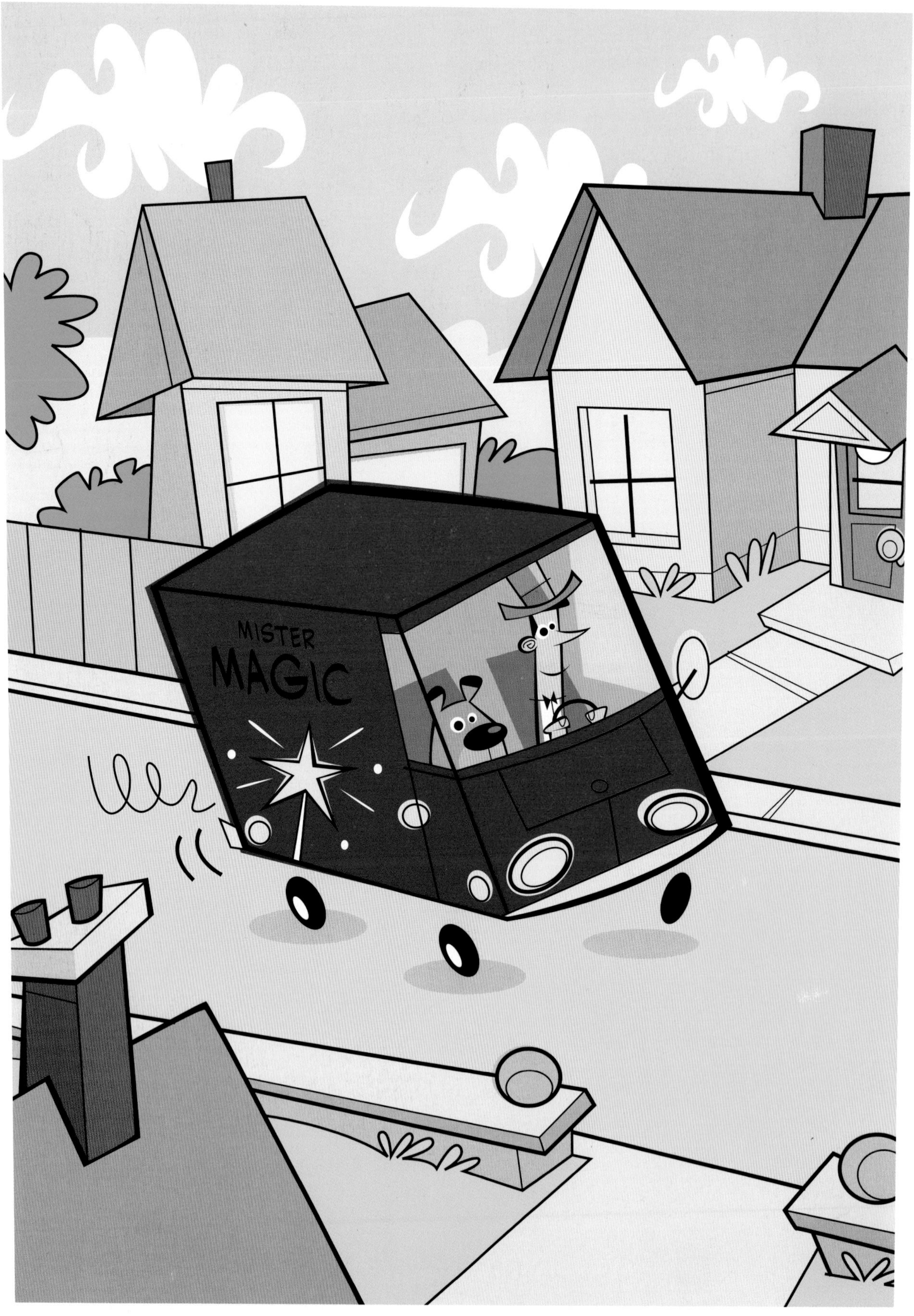
MISTER
MAGIC

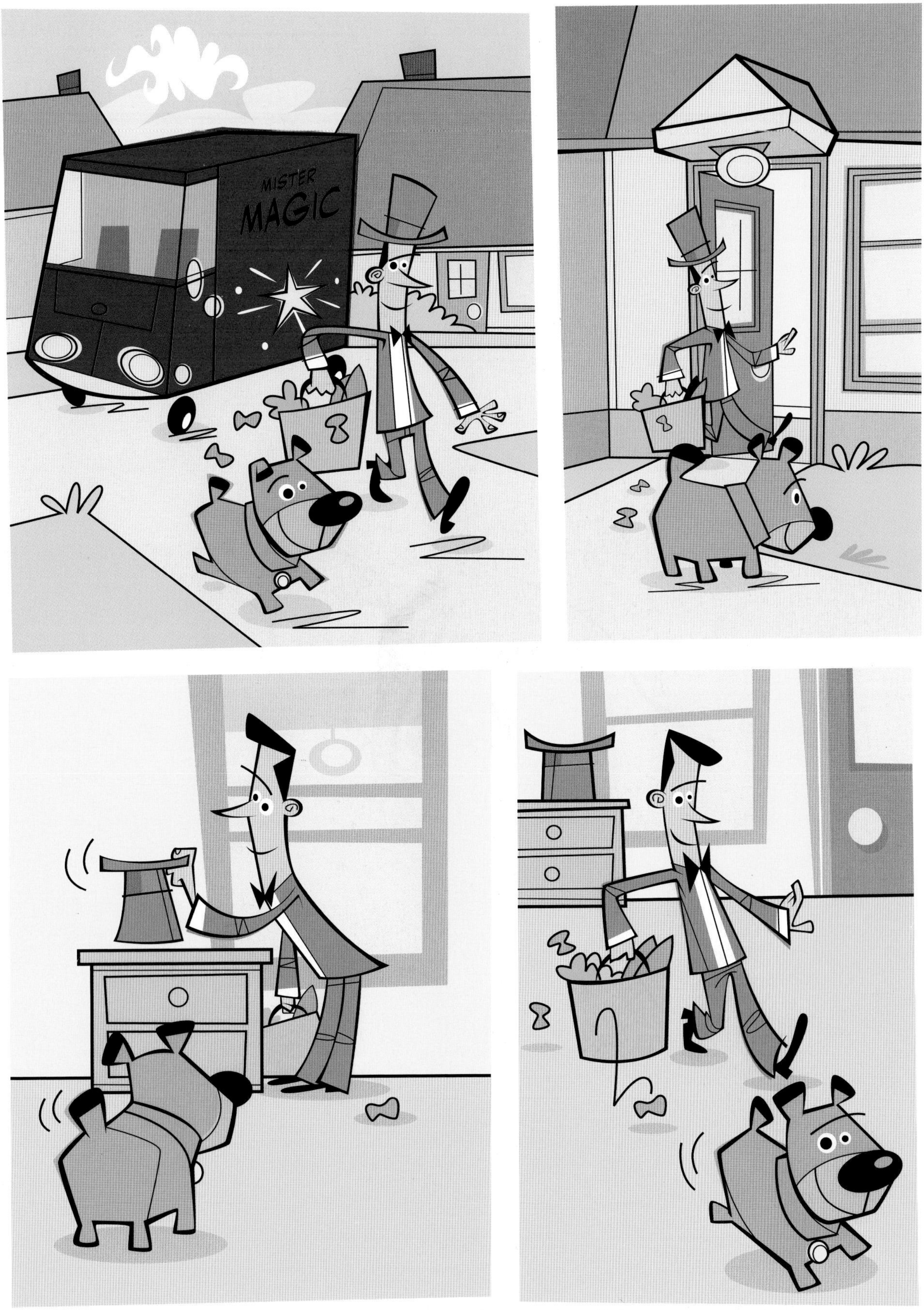
MISTER
MAGIC

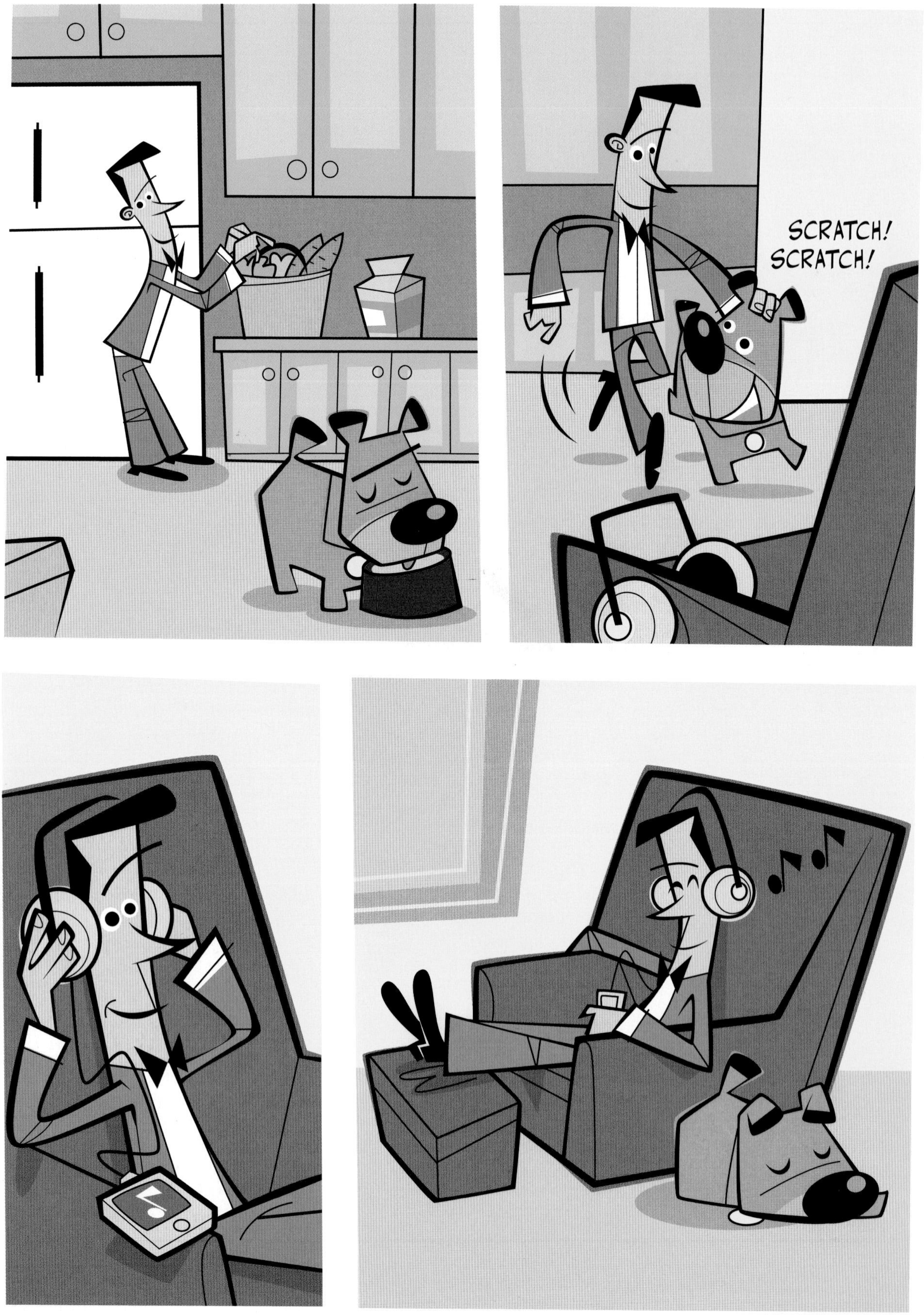
SCRATCH!
SCRATCH!

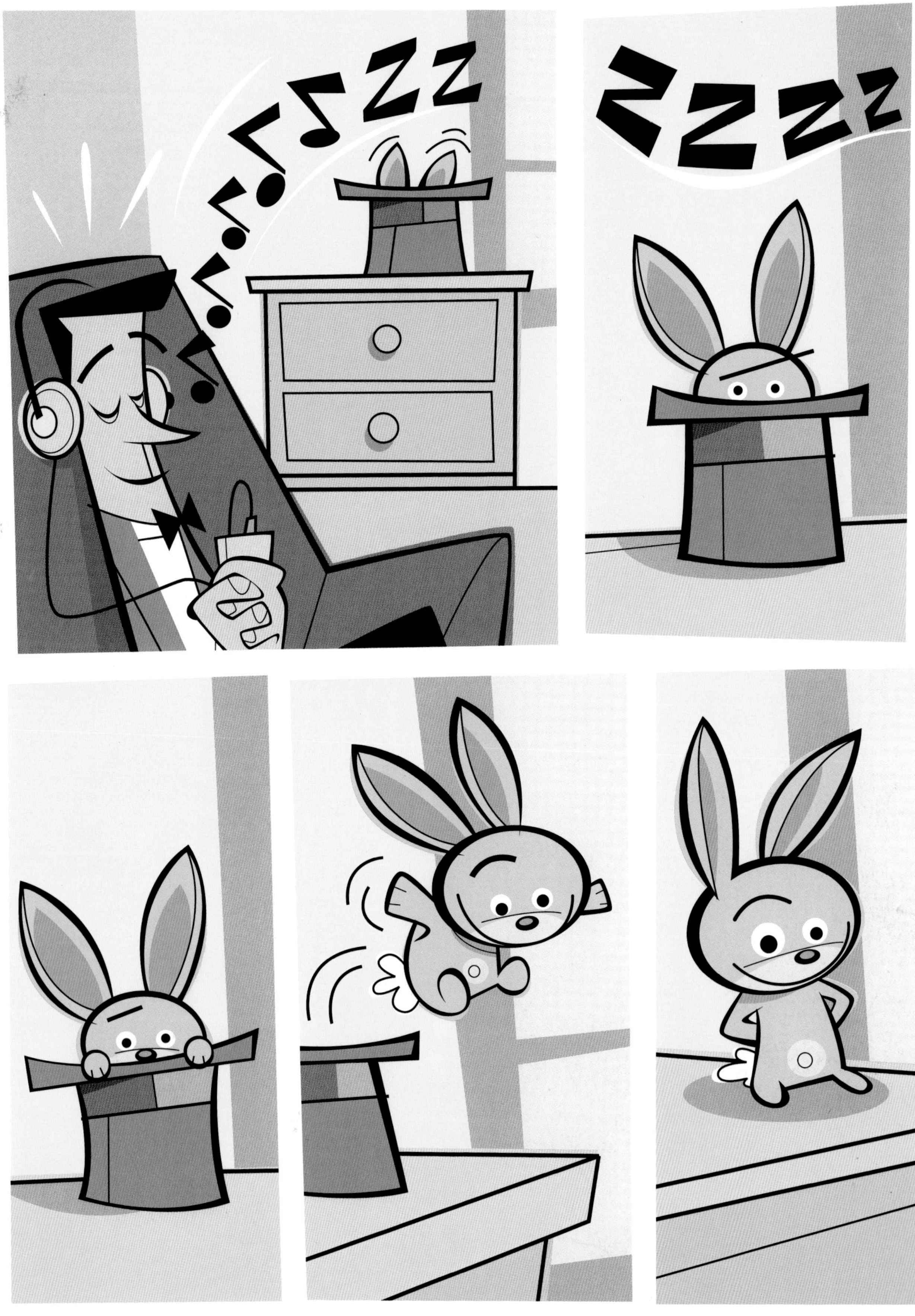

ZZZ
ZZZZ

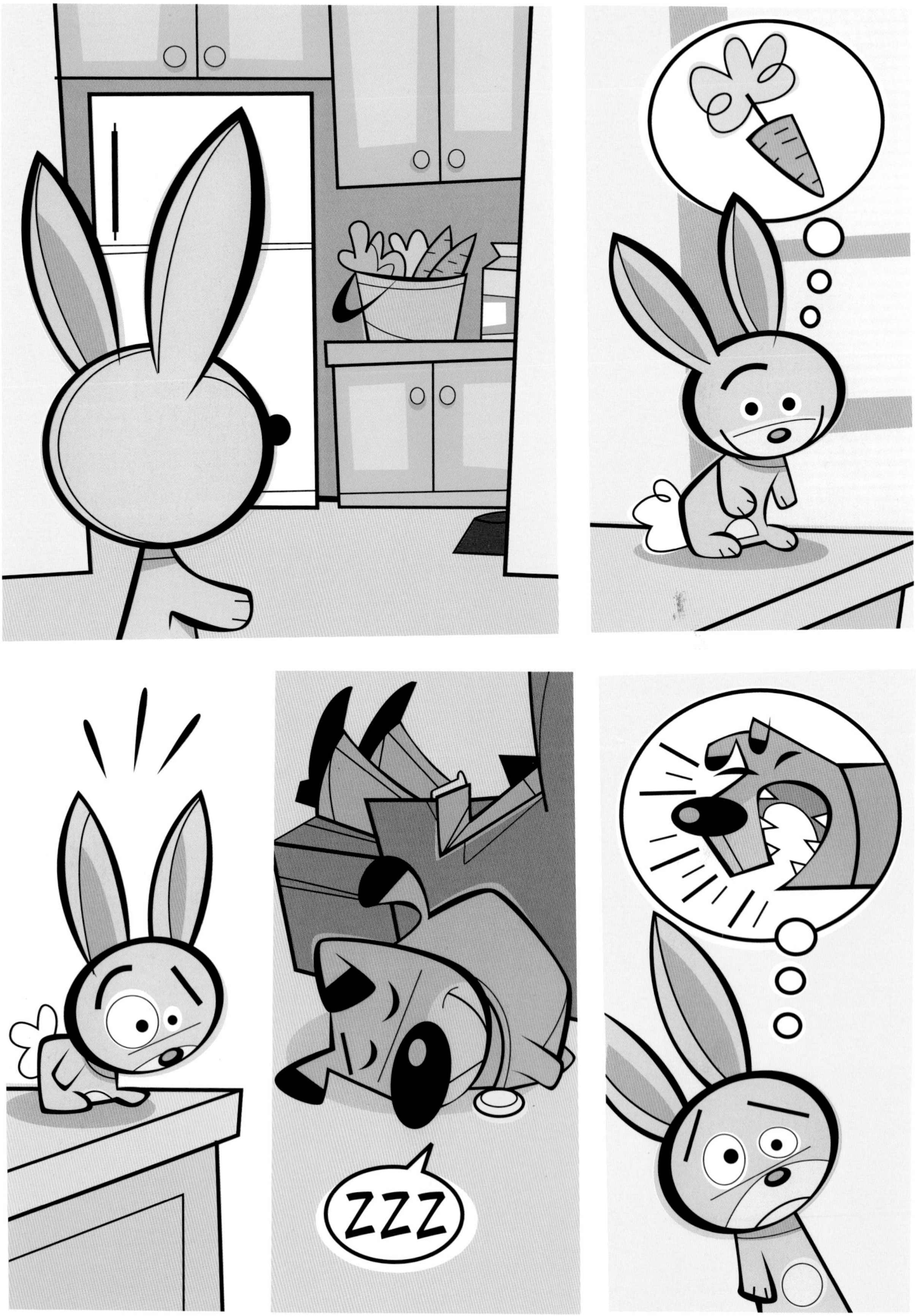
ZZZ

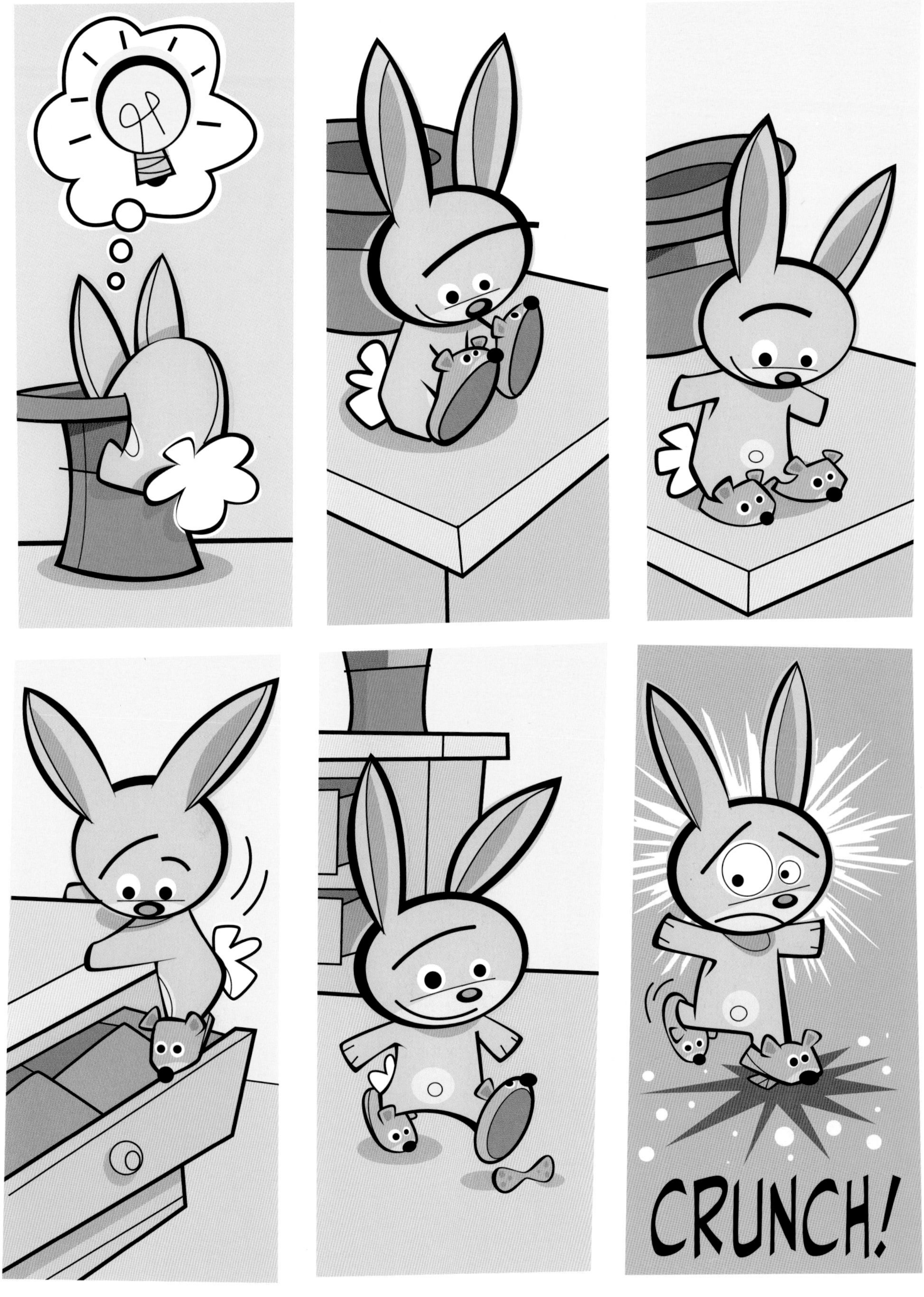
CRUNCH!

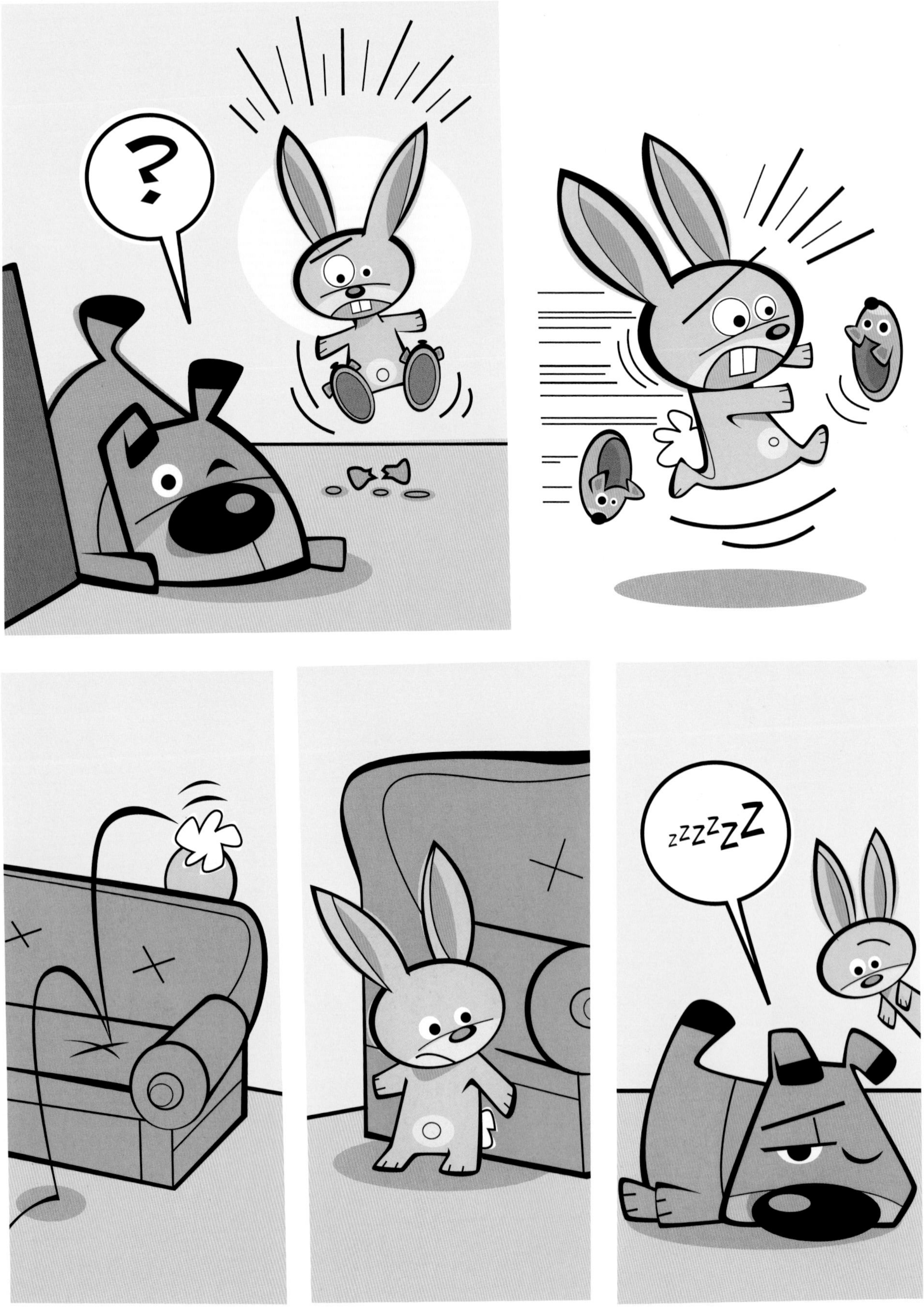
?
zzzzzZ

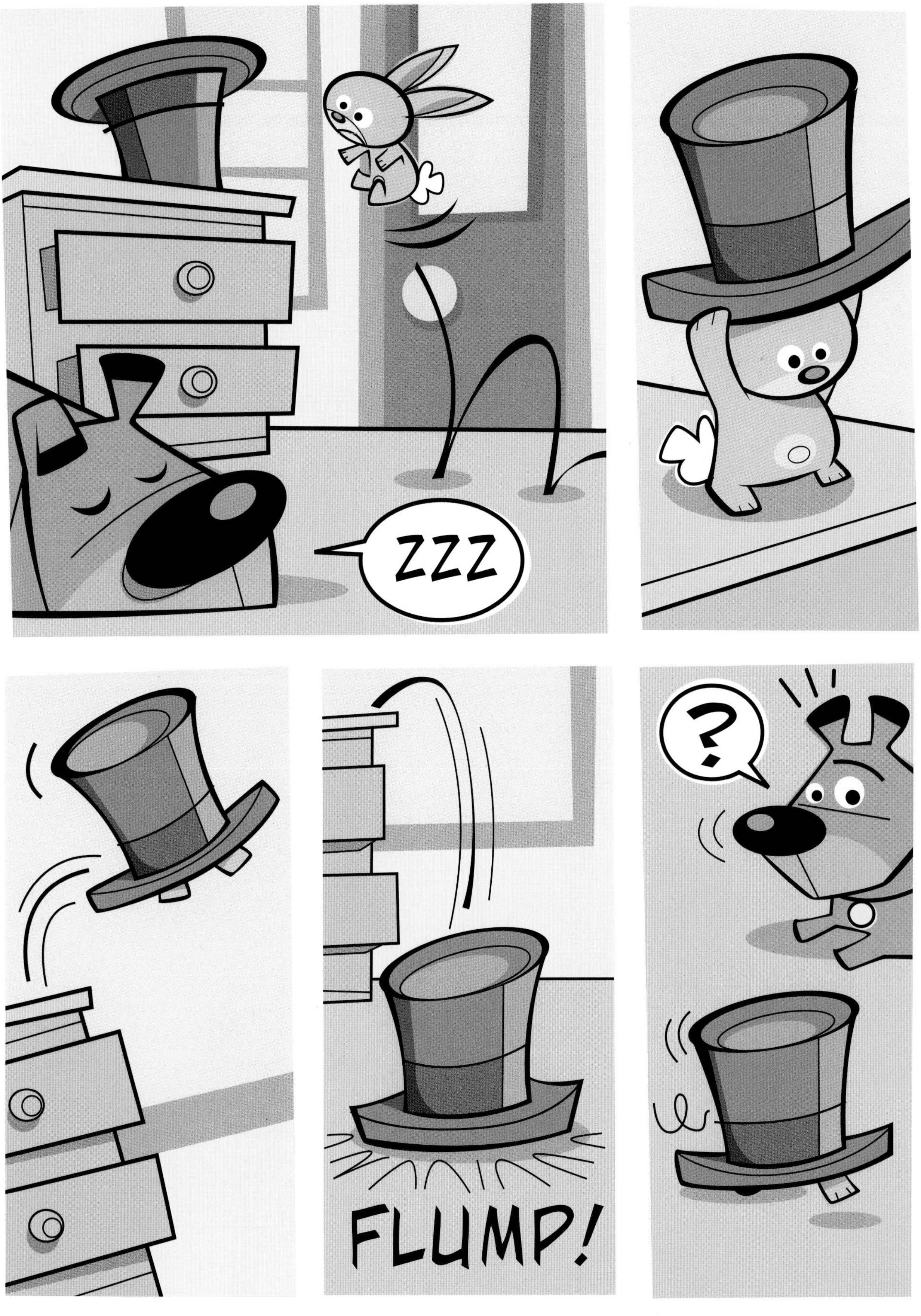
ZZZ
FLUMP!
?

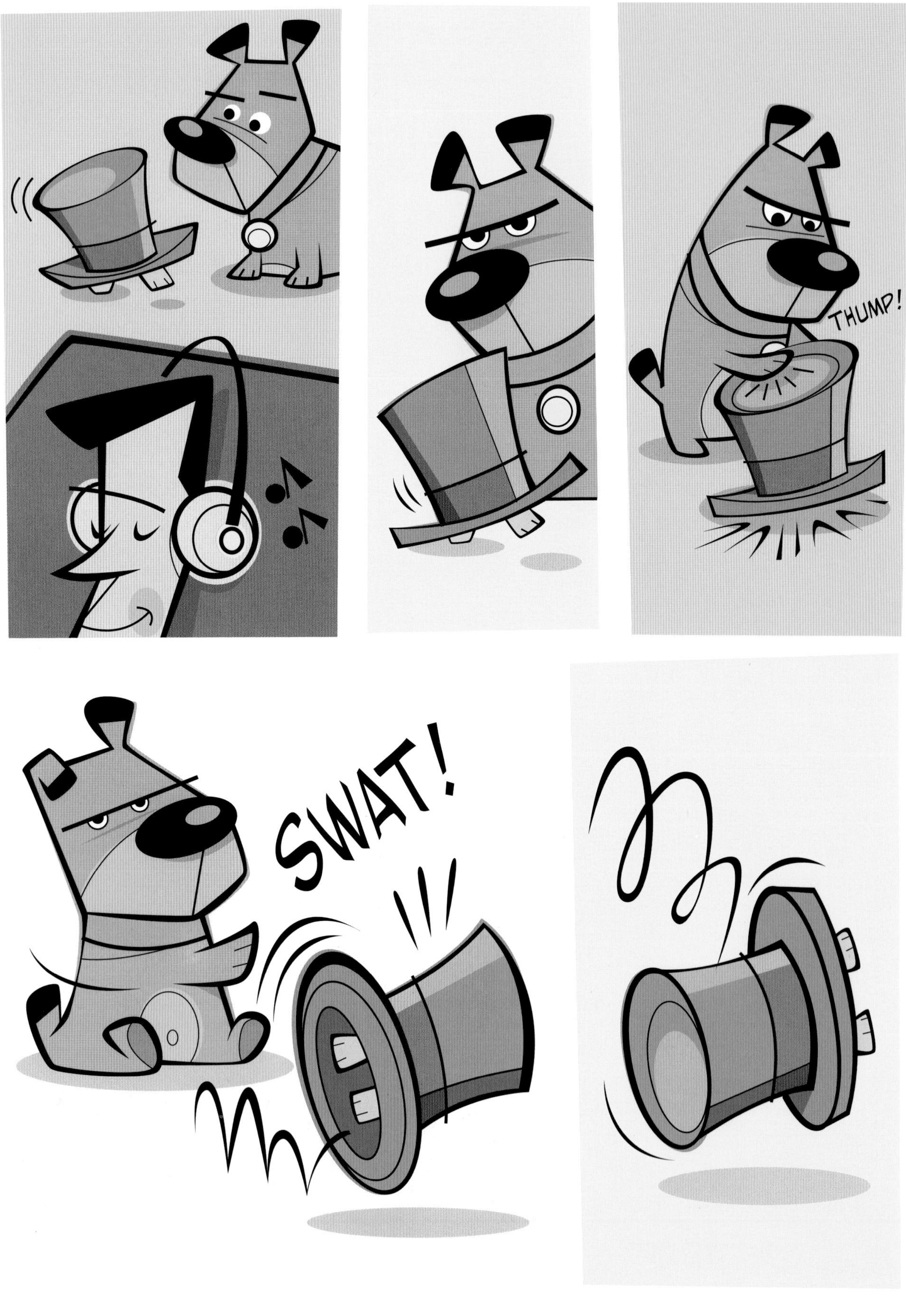
THUMP!
SWAT!

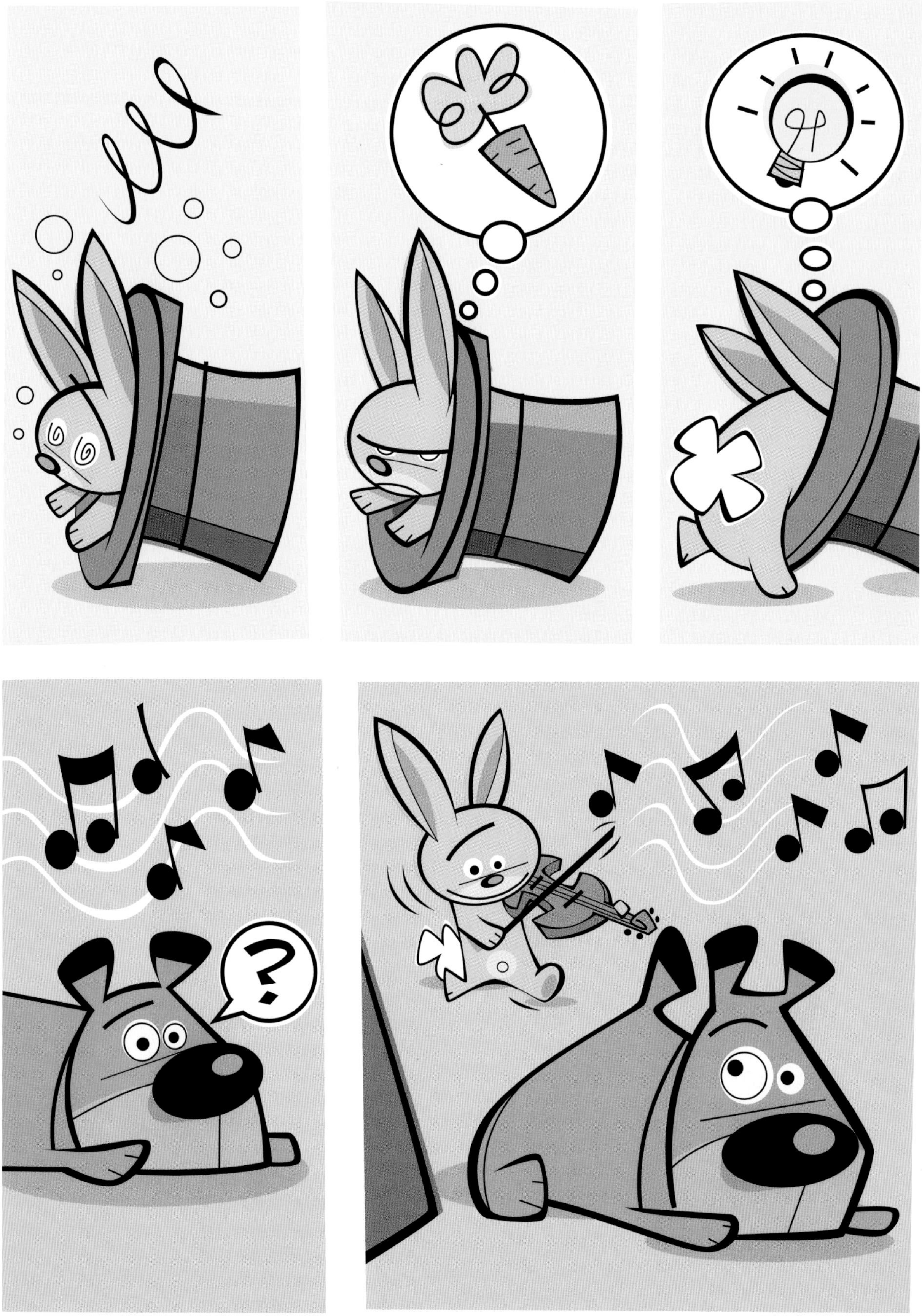
?

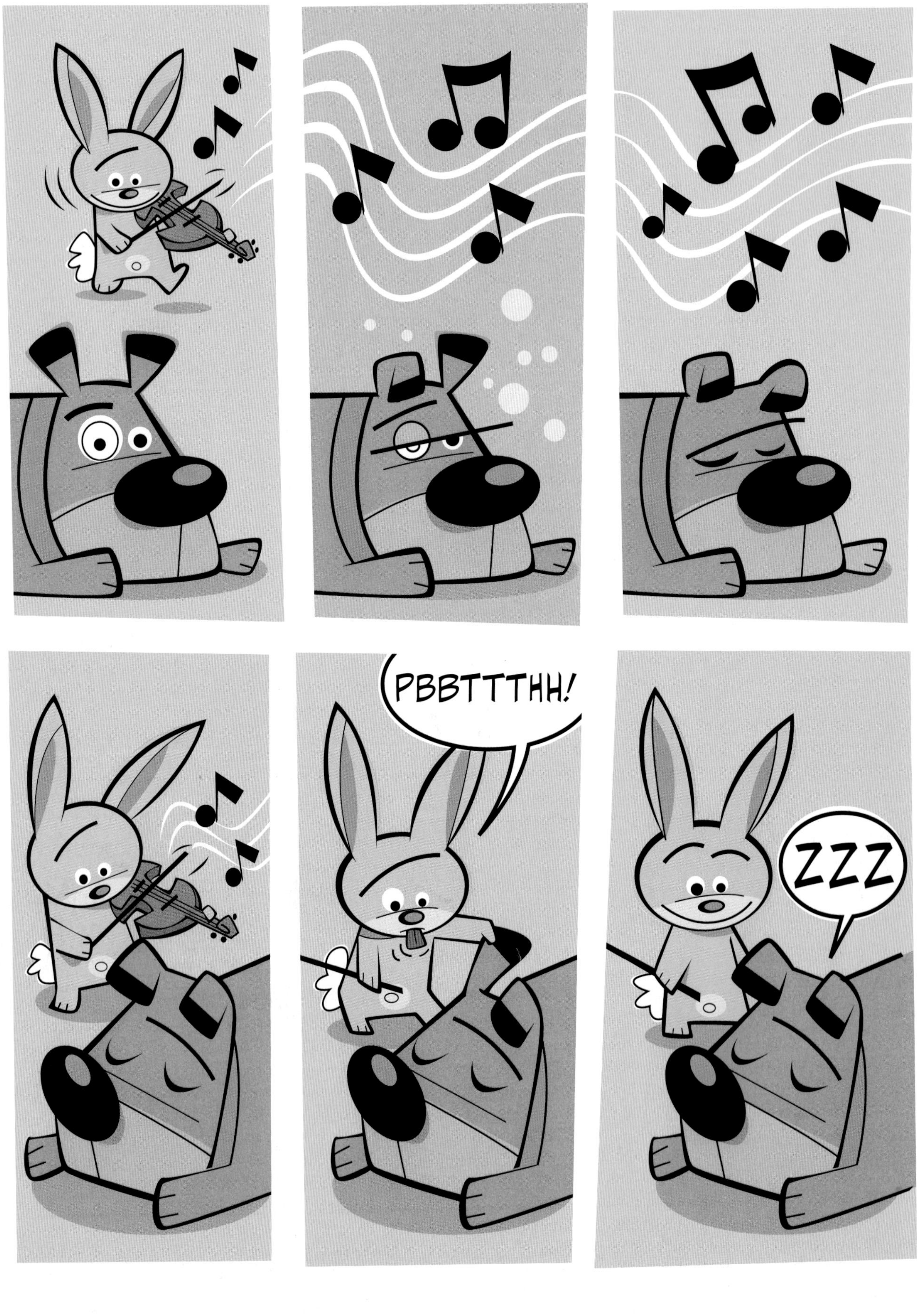
PBBTTTHH!
ZZZ

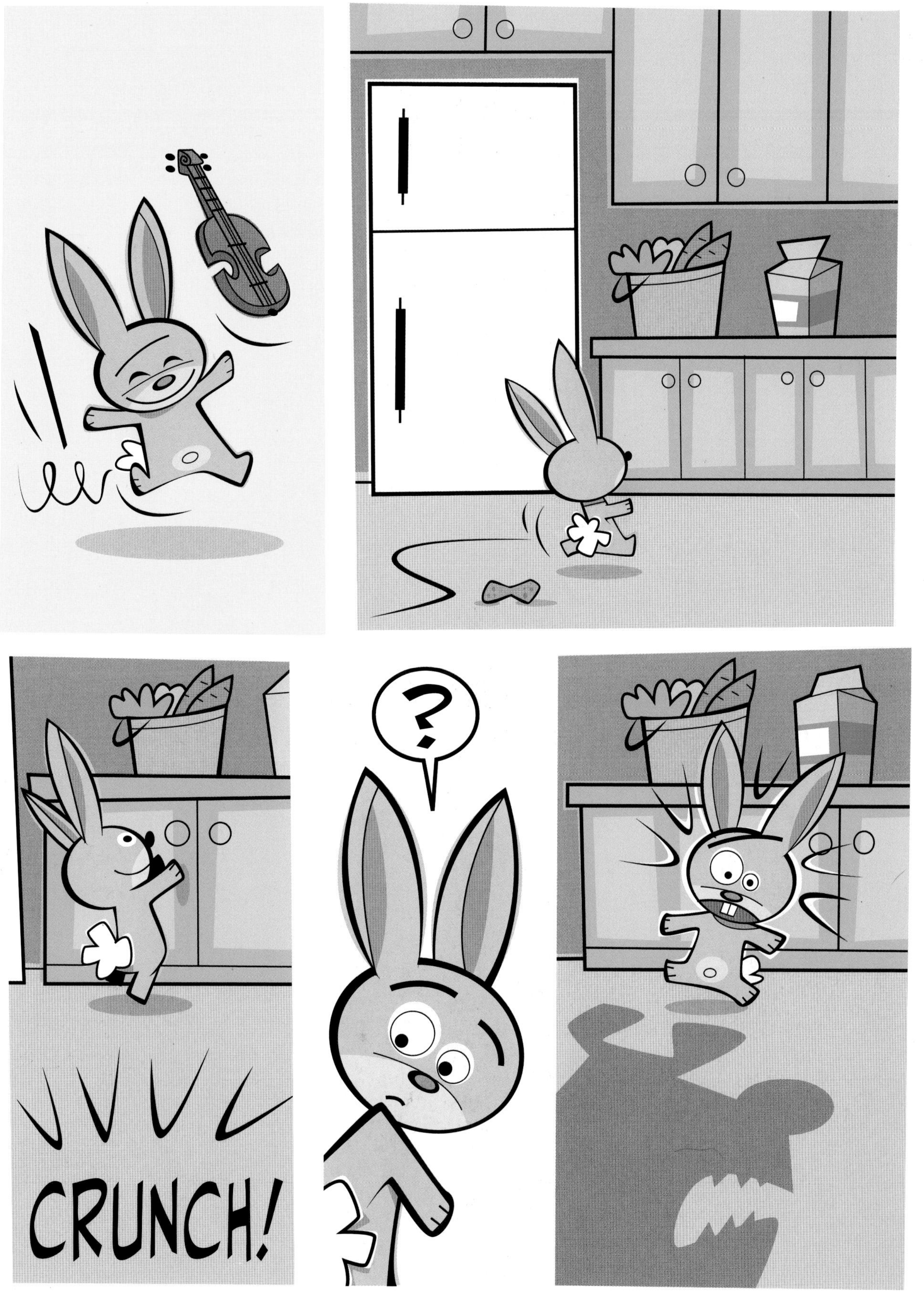
CRUNCH!
?

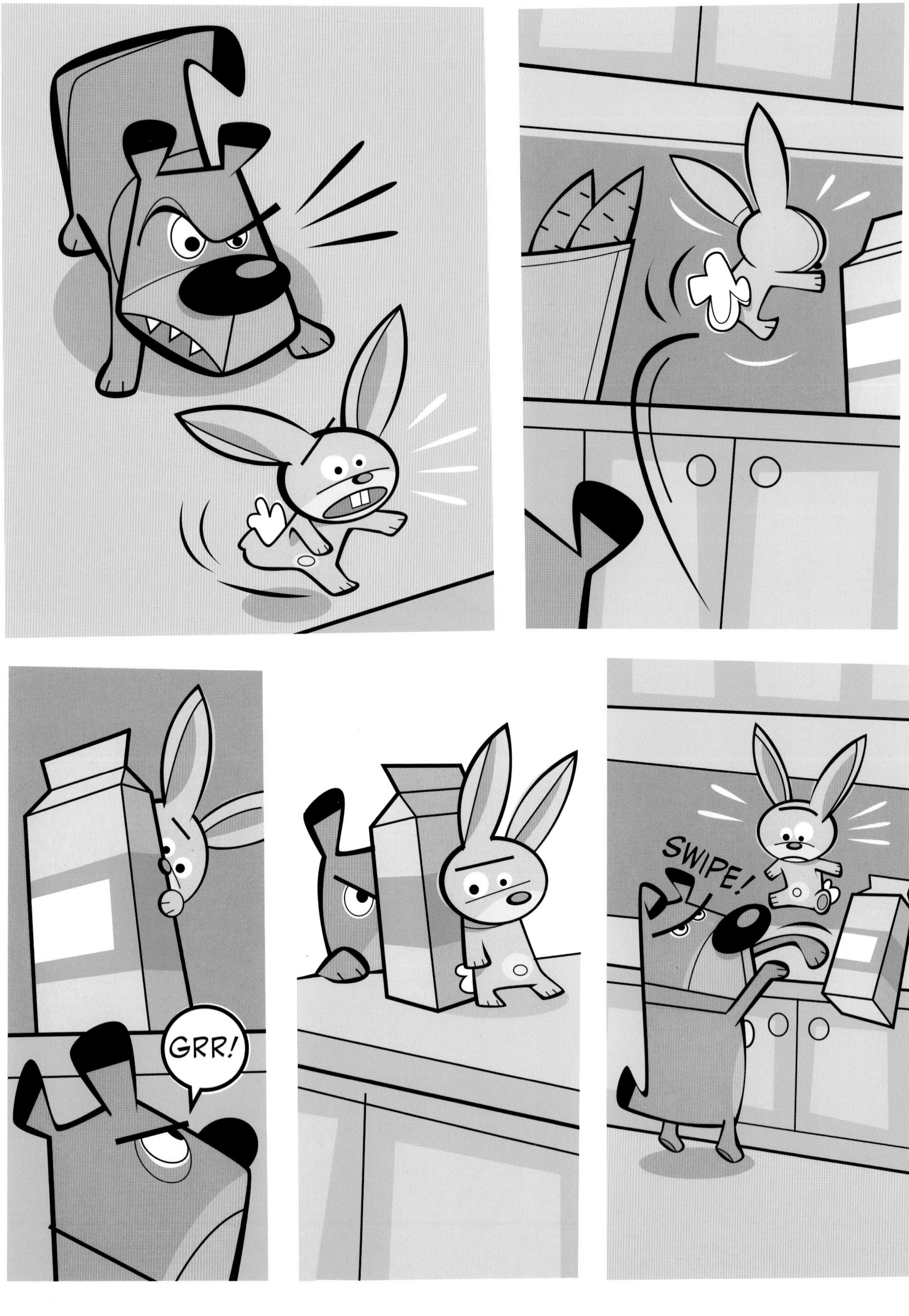
GRR!
SWIPE!

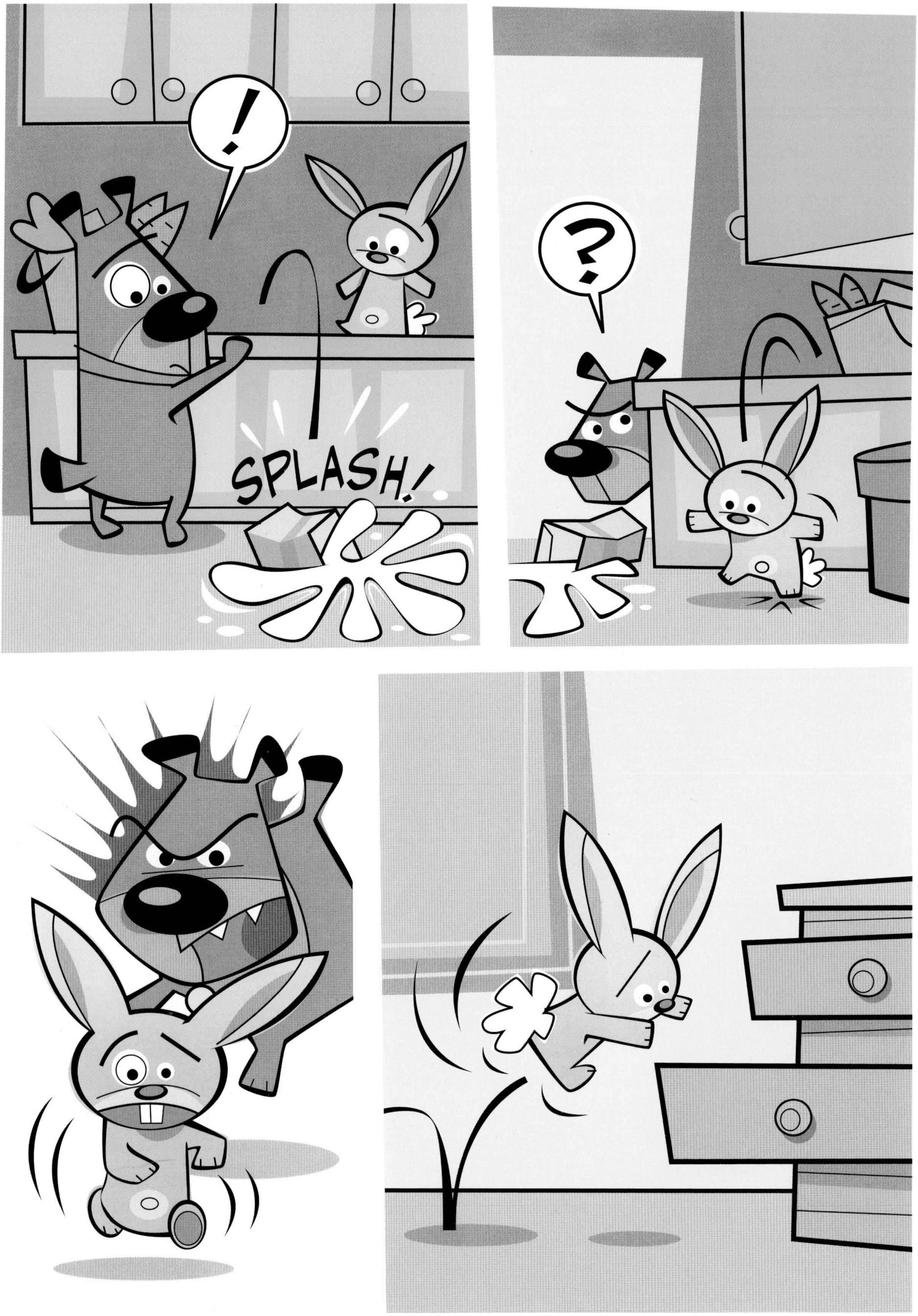
!
SPLASH!
?

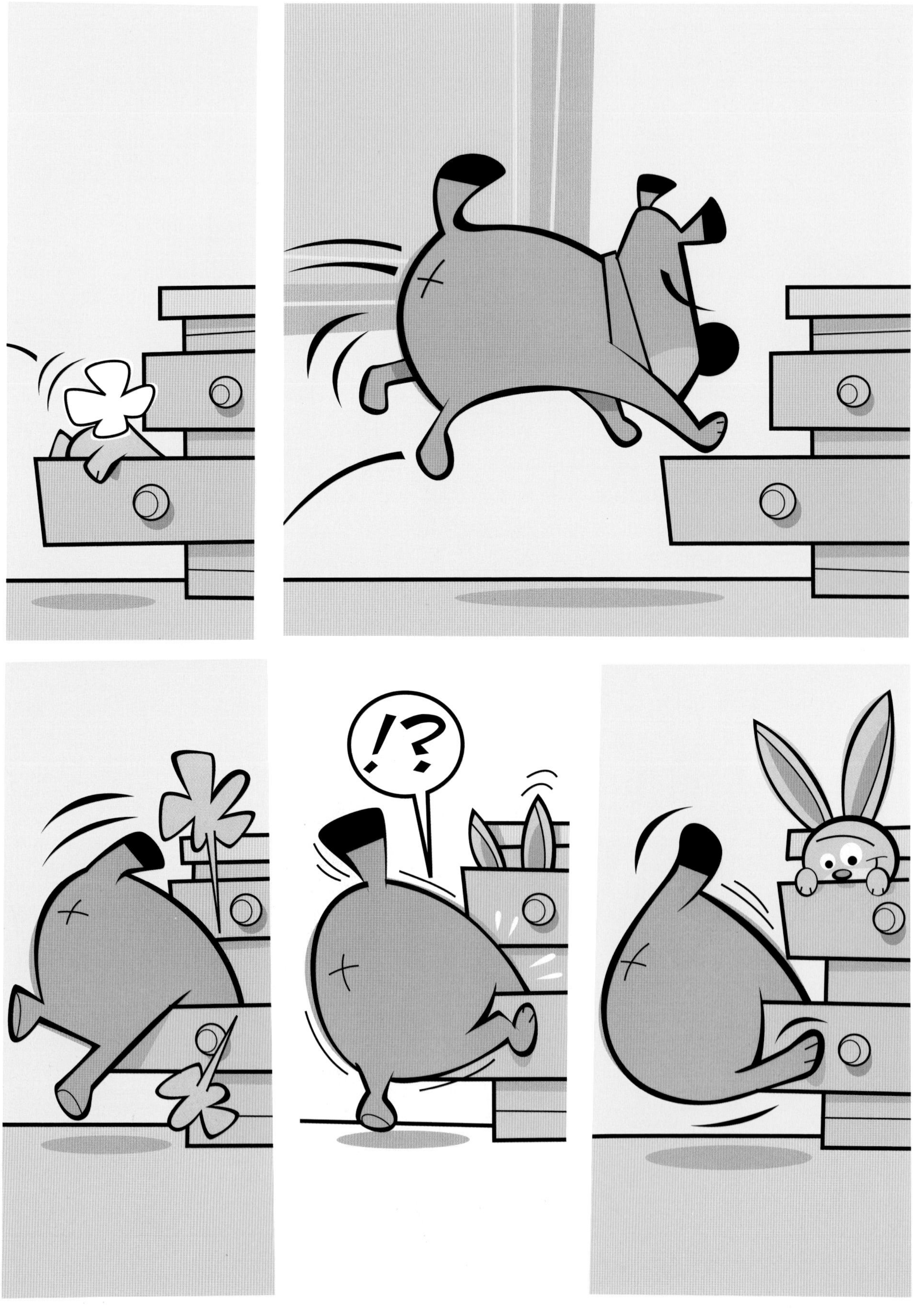
!?

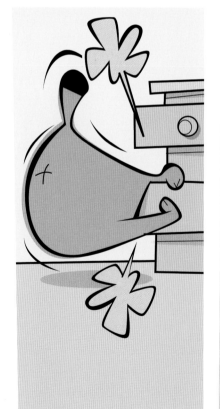

POP!

GRRR!

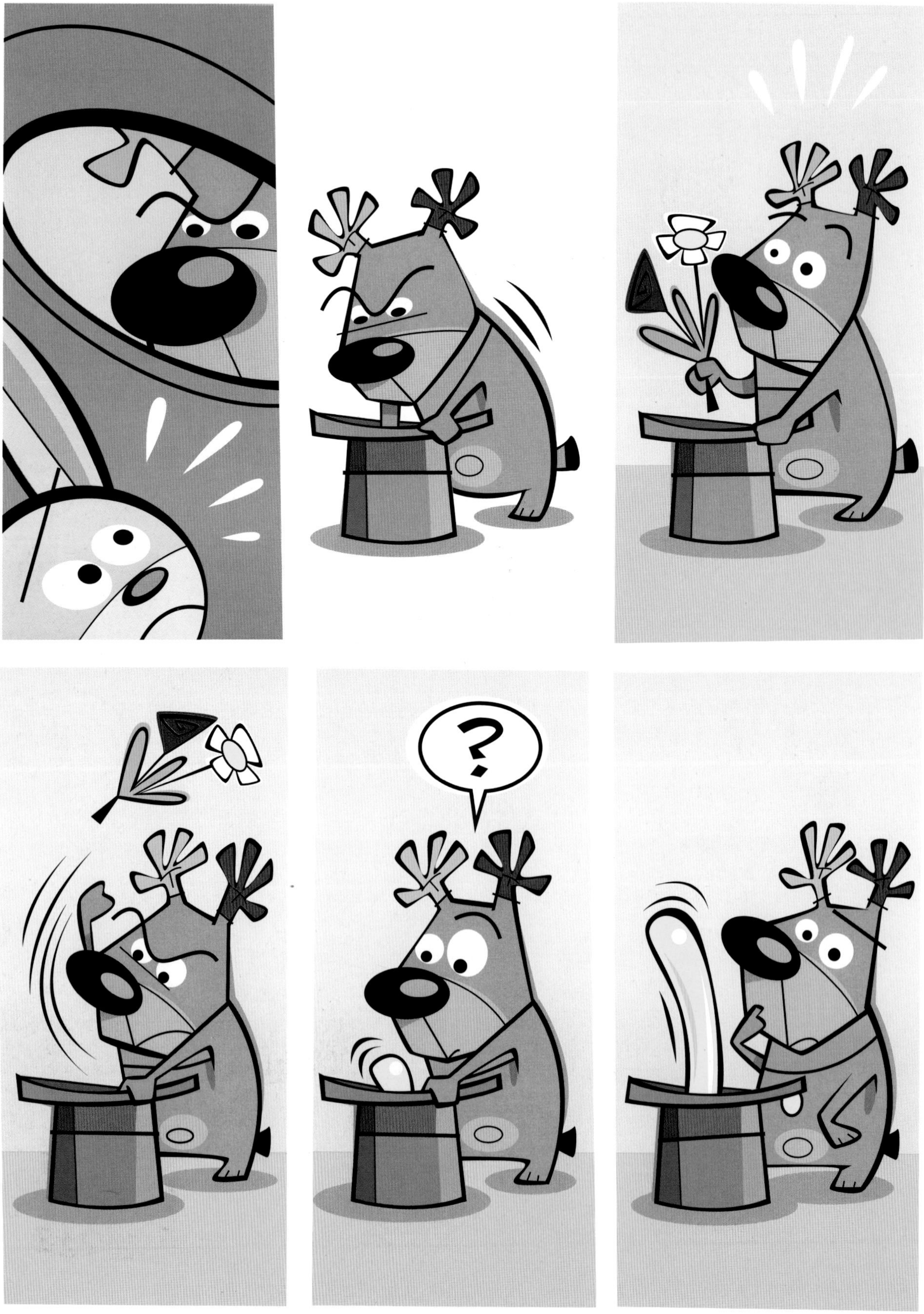
?

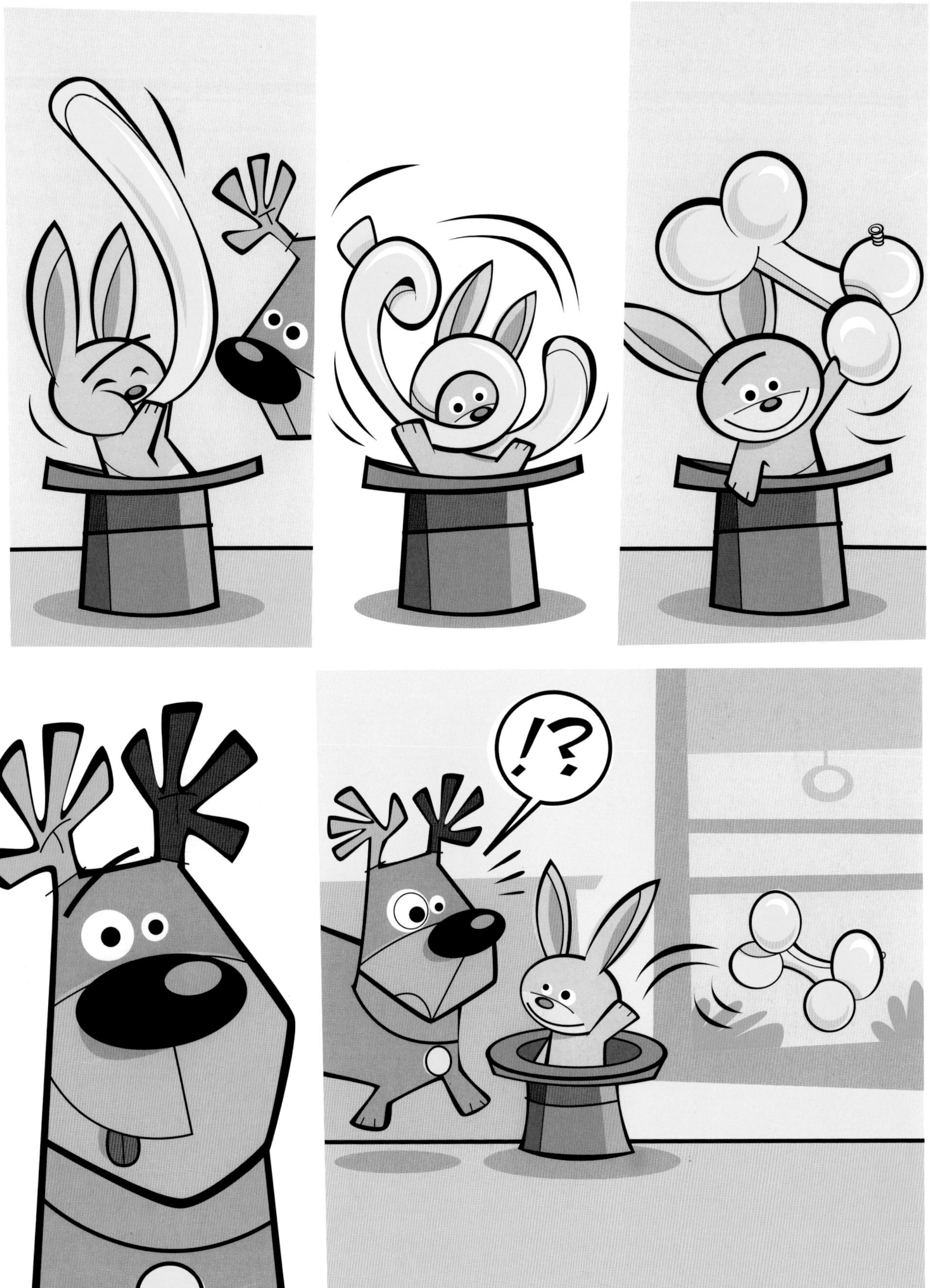
!?

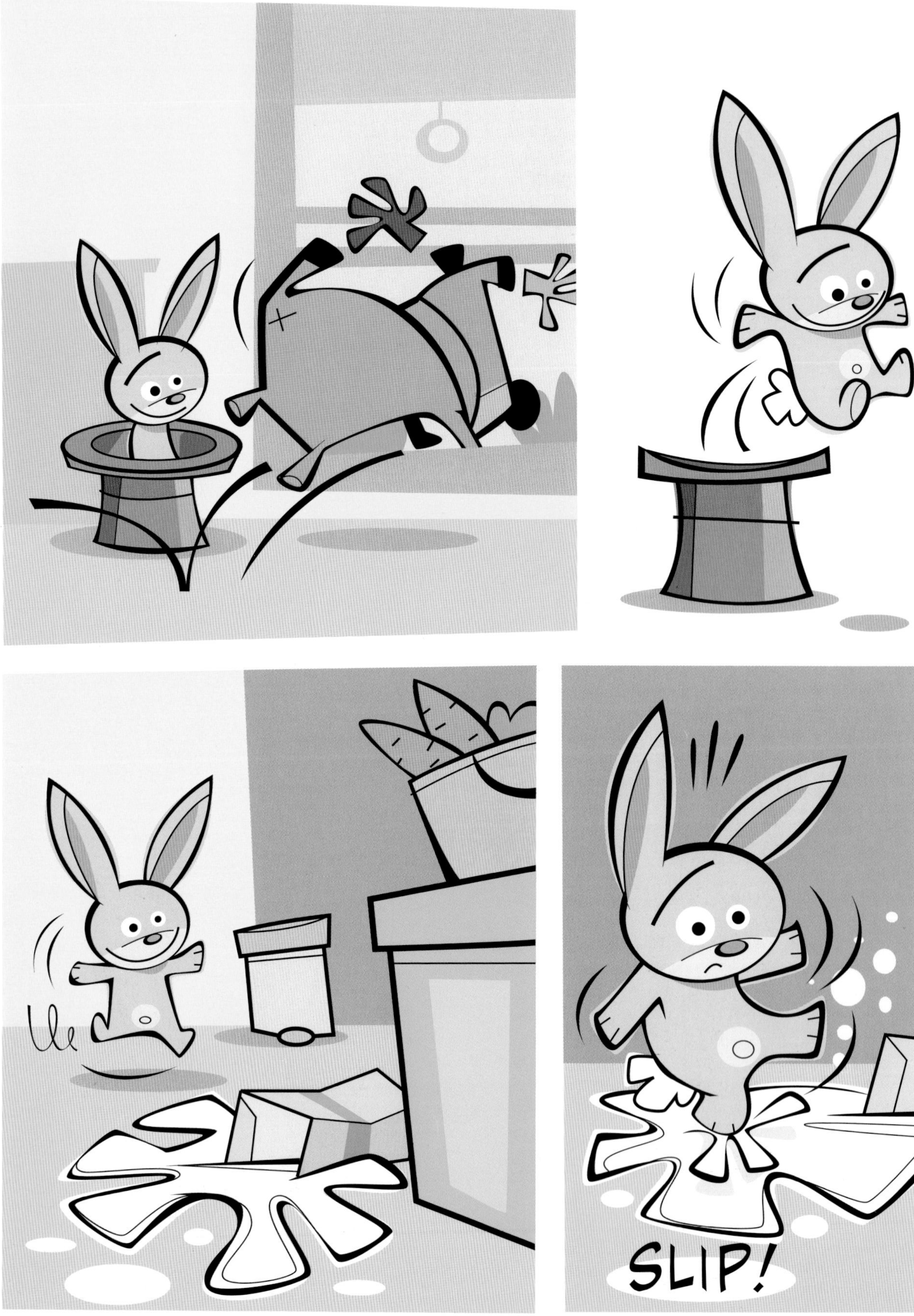
SLIP!

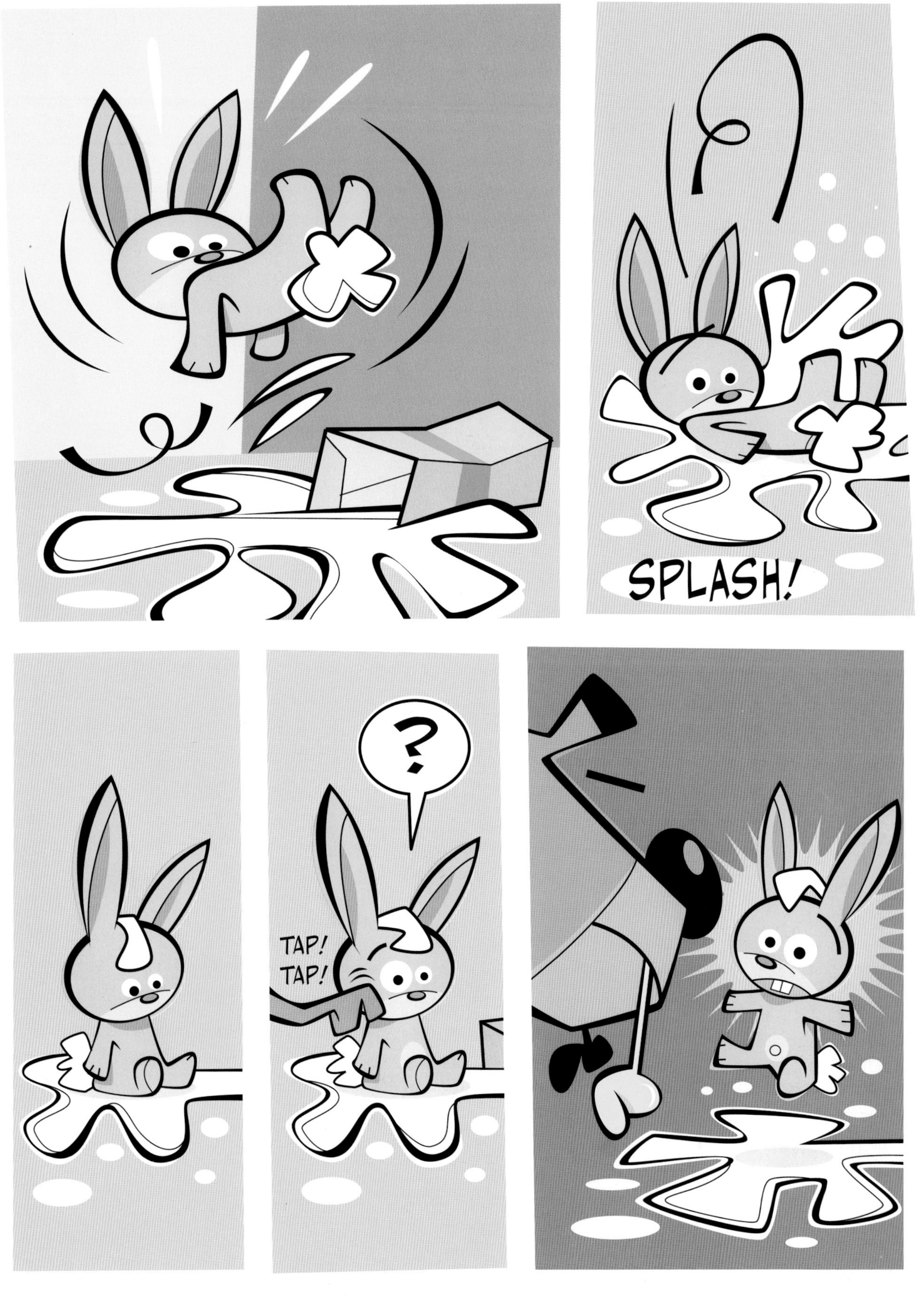
SPLASH!
?
TAP! TAP!

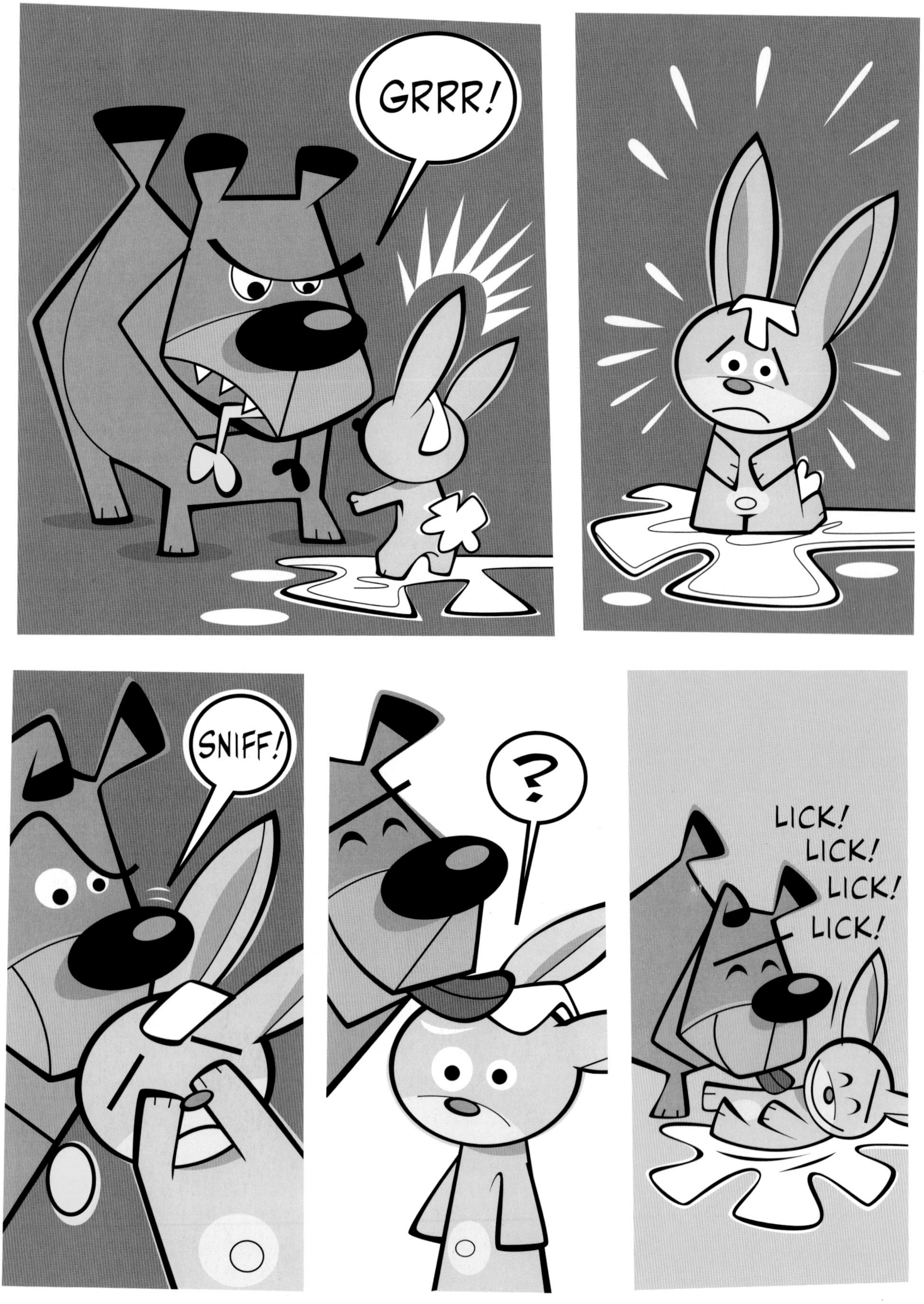
GRRR!
SNIFF!
?
LICK!
LICK!
LICK!
LICK!

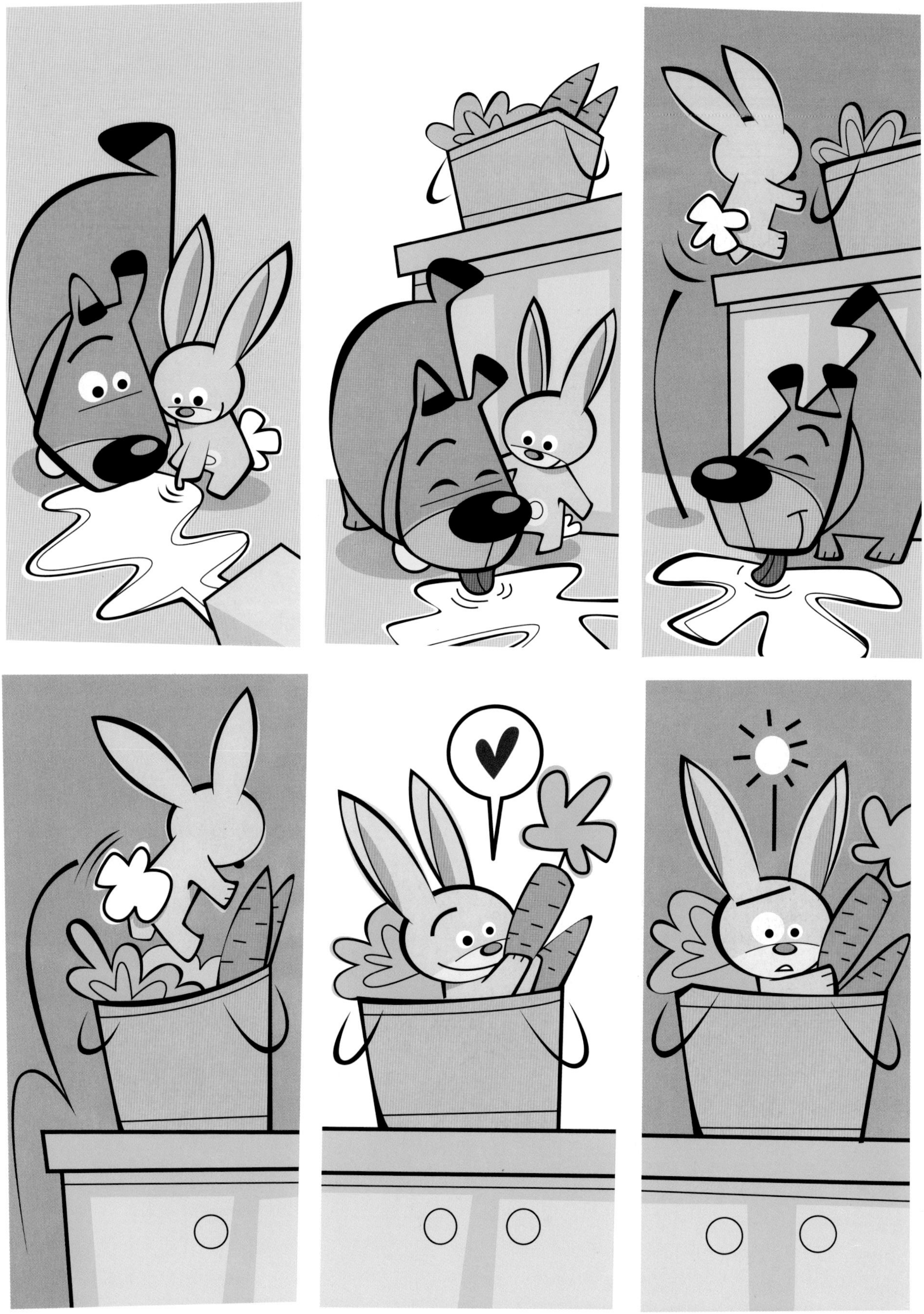

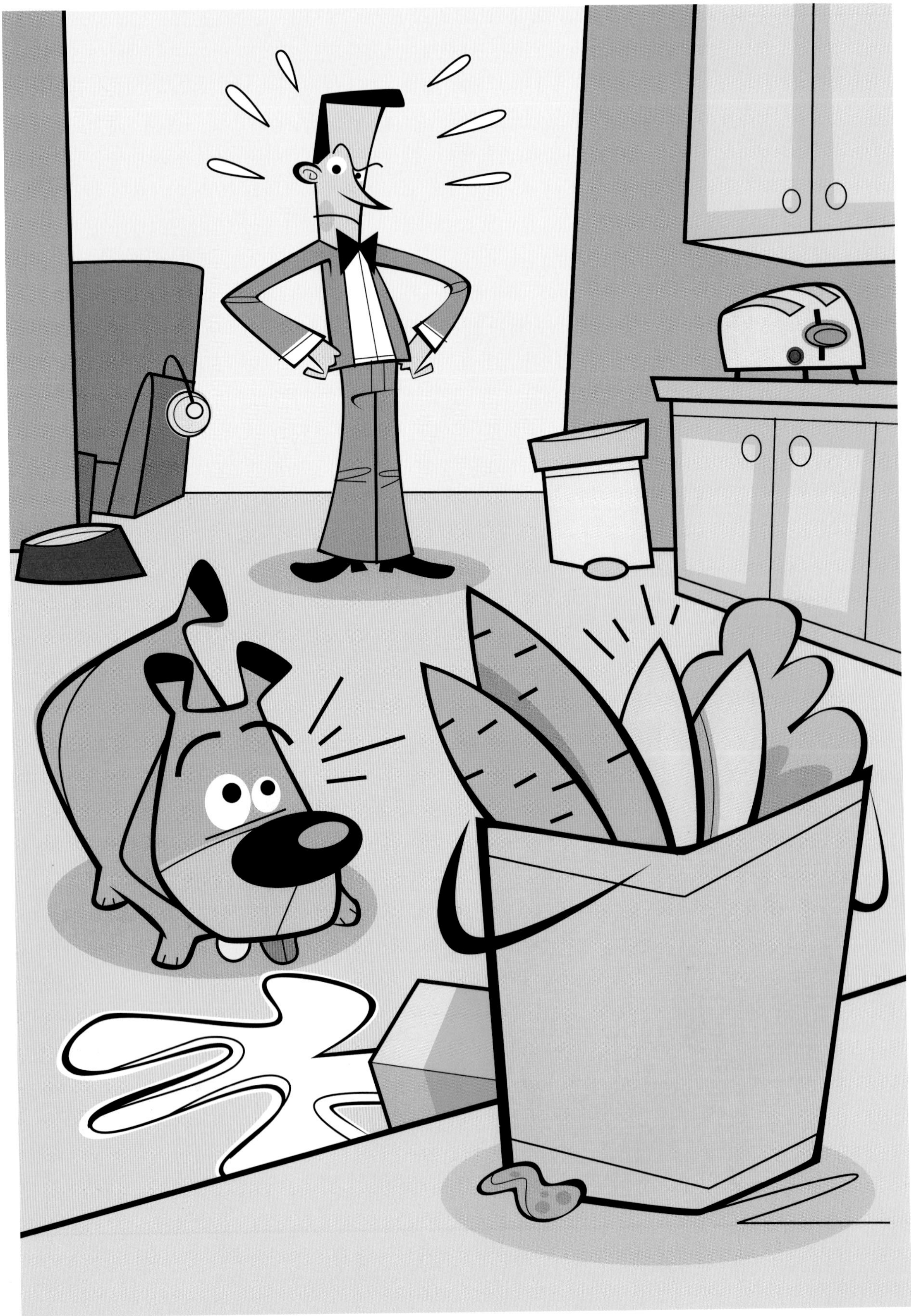

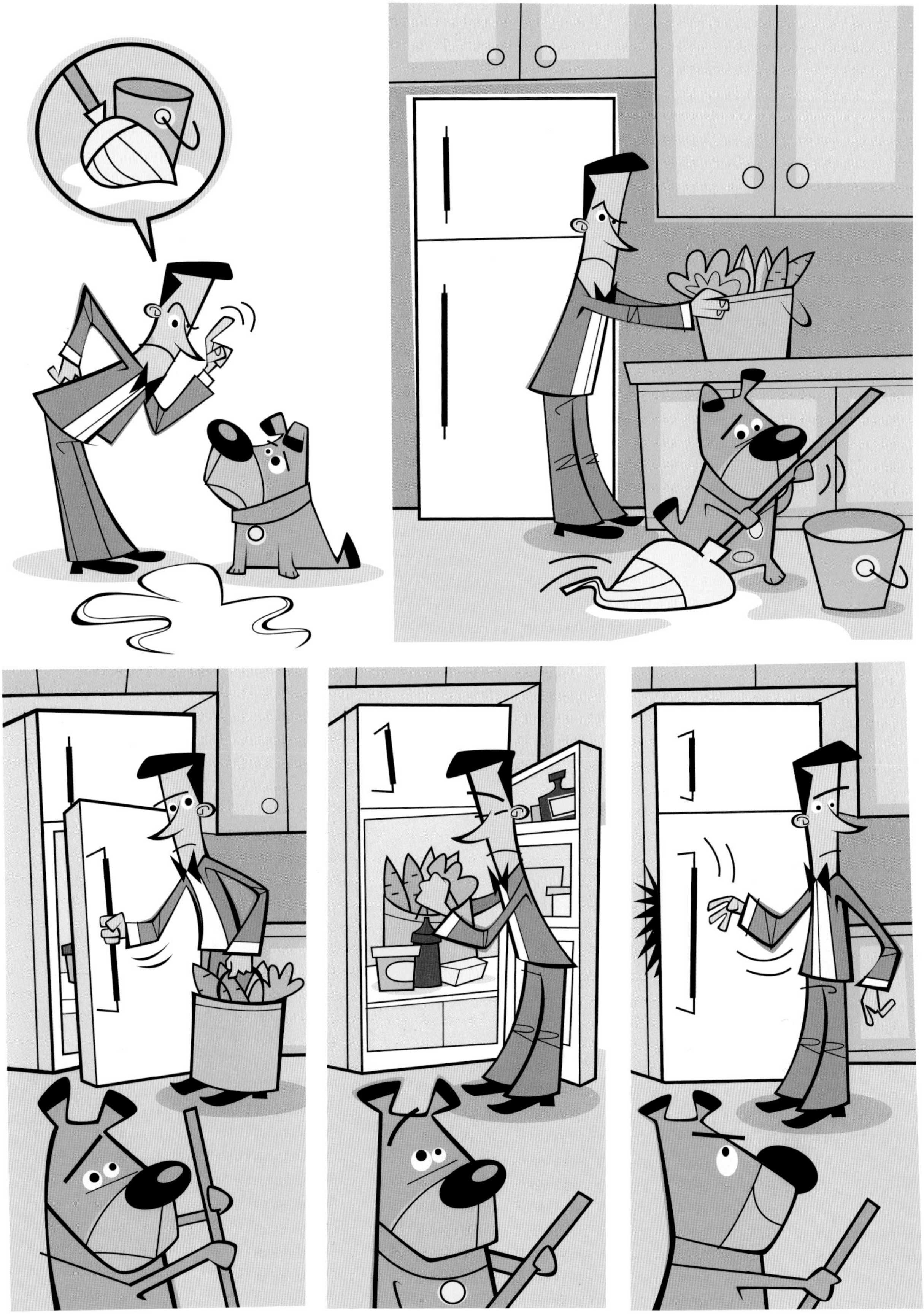

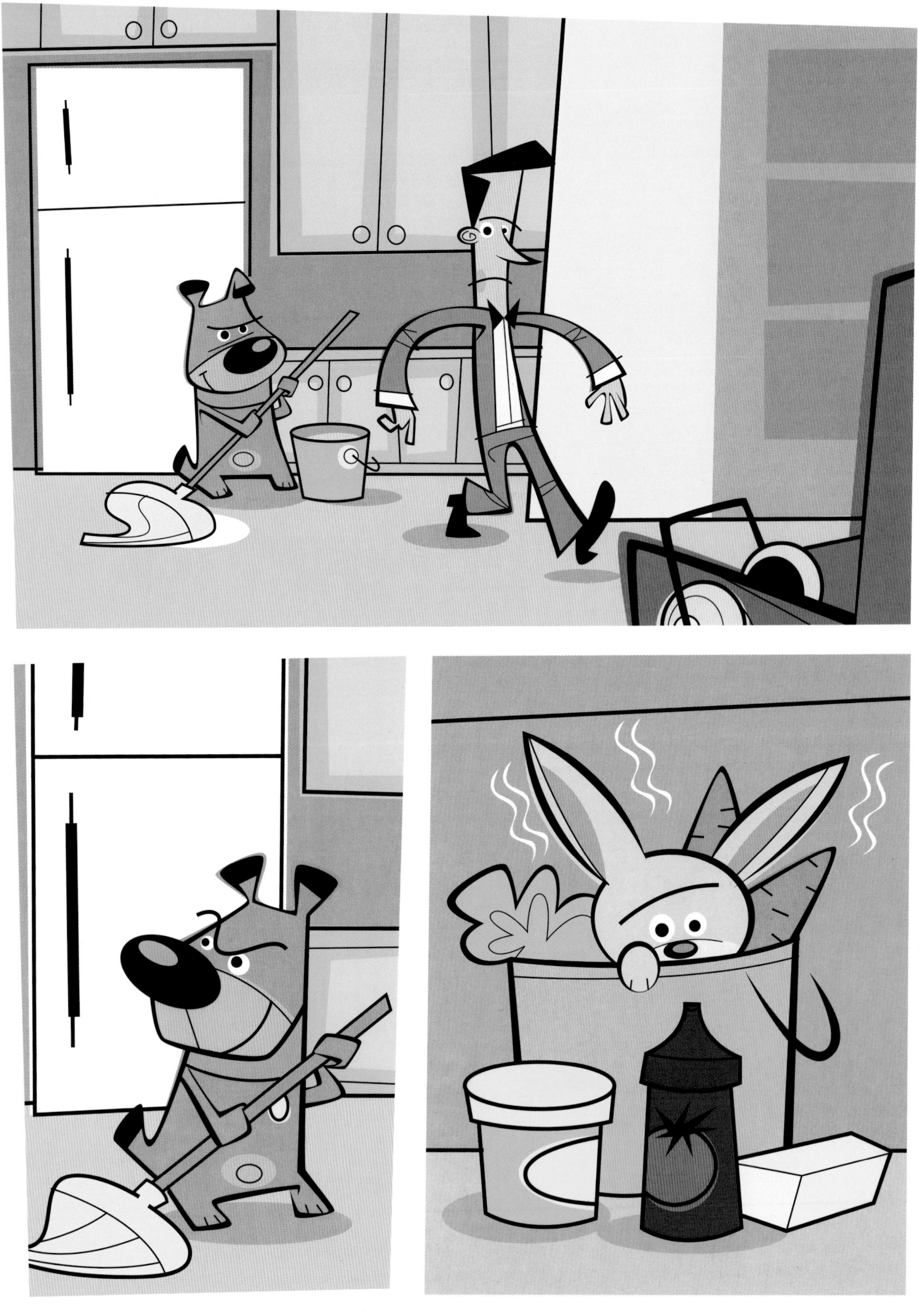

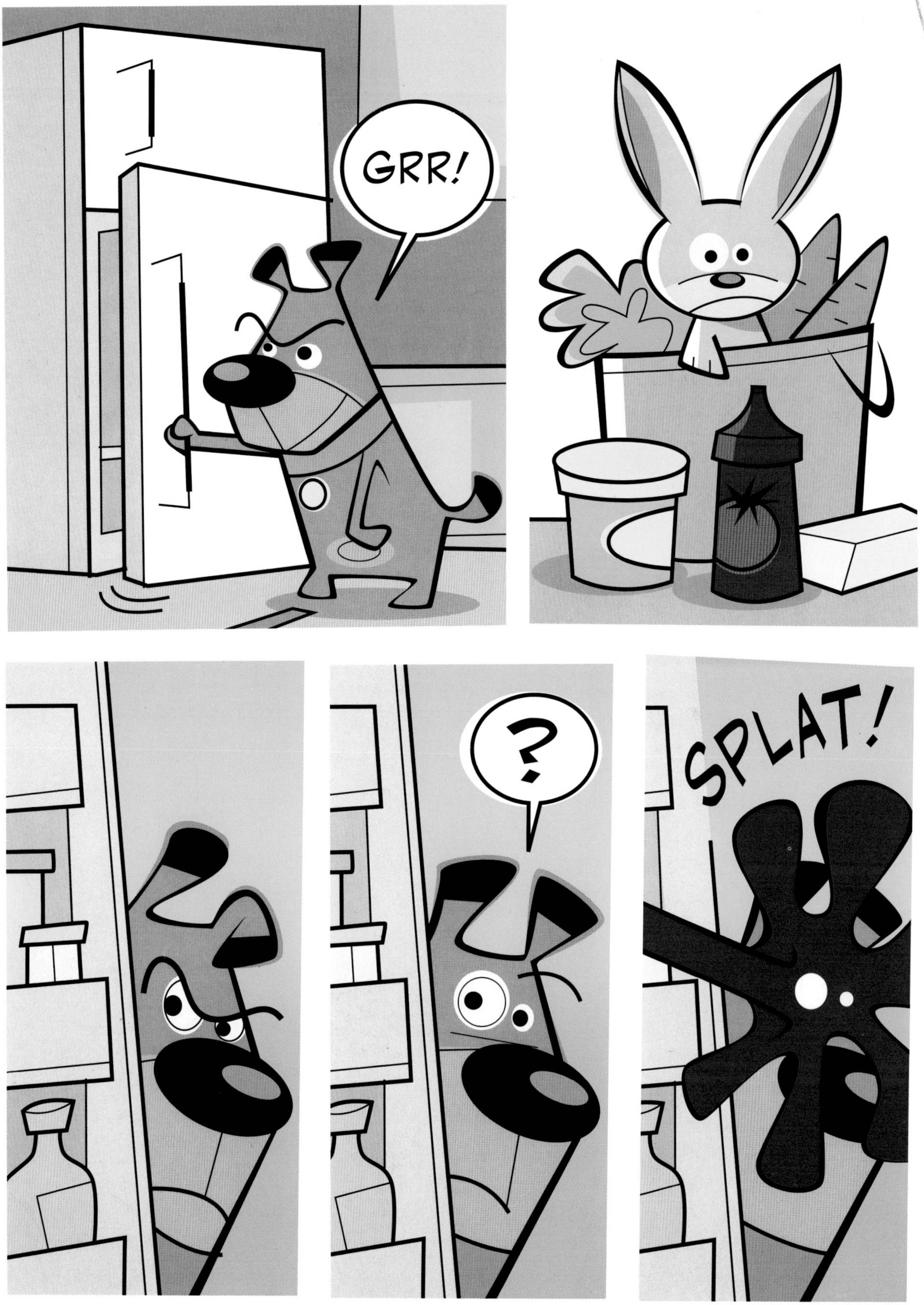
GRR!
?
SPLAT!

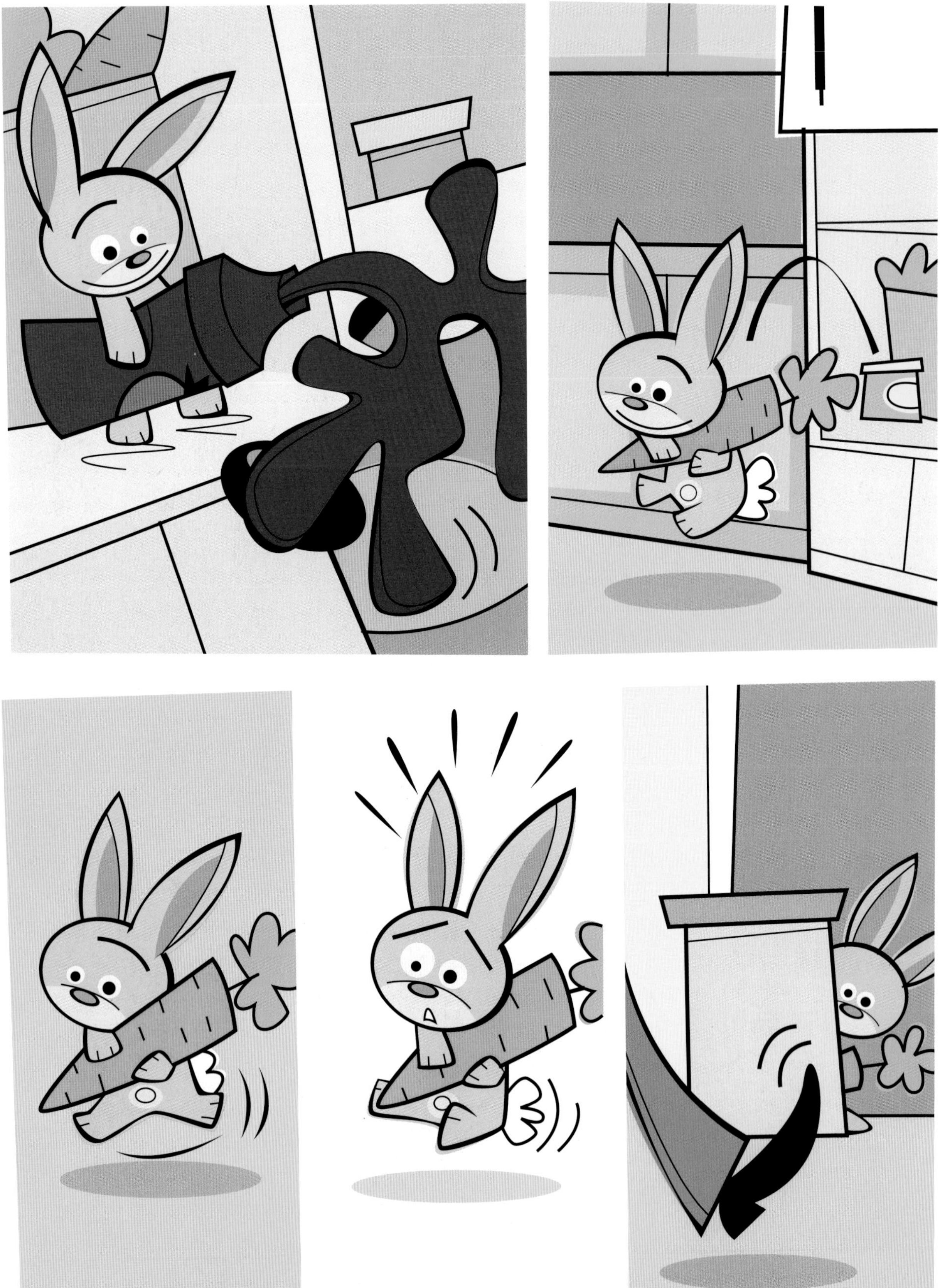

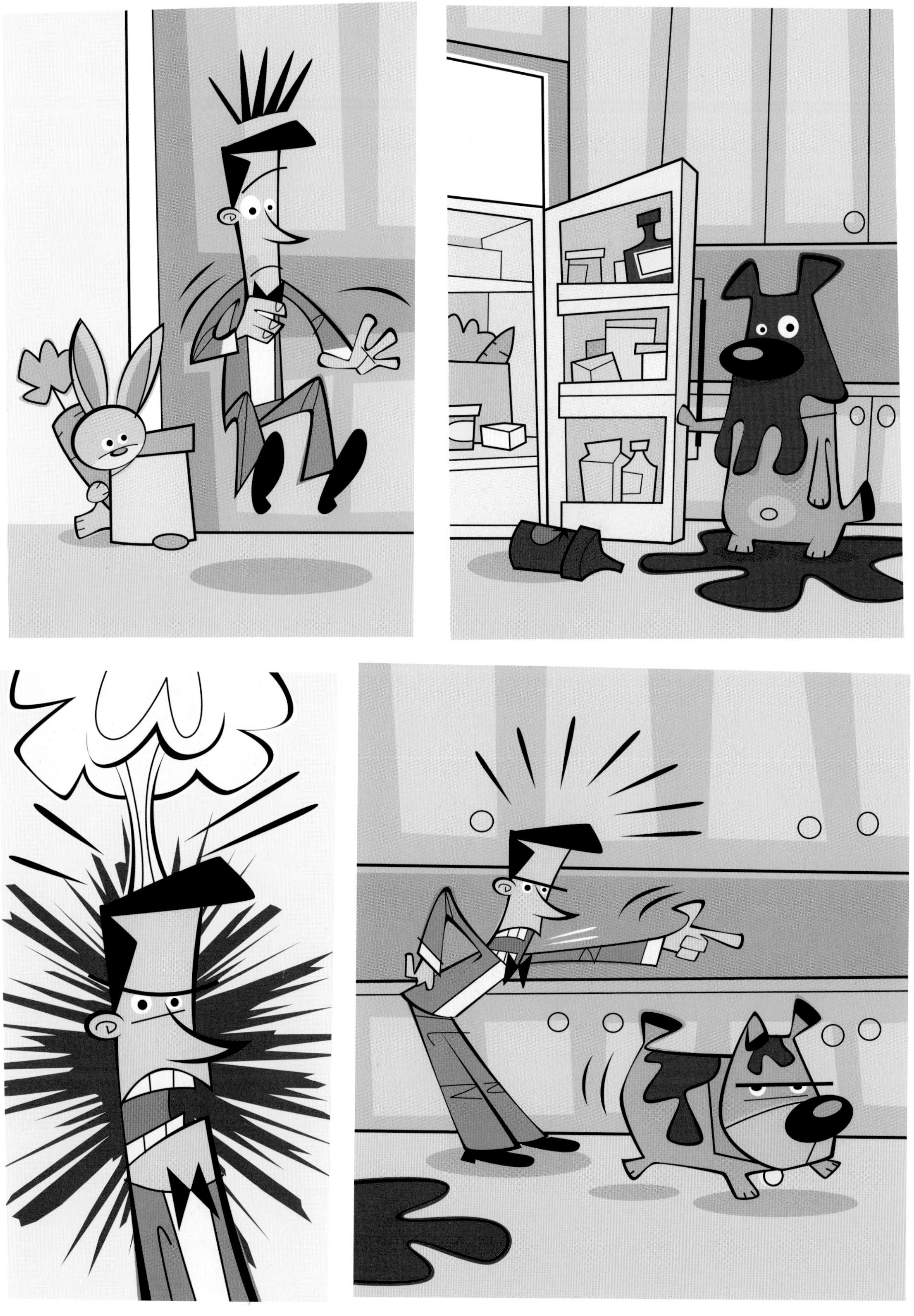

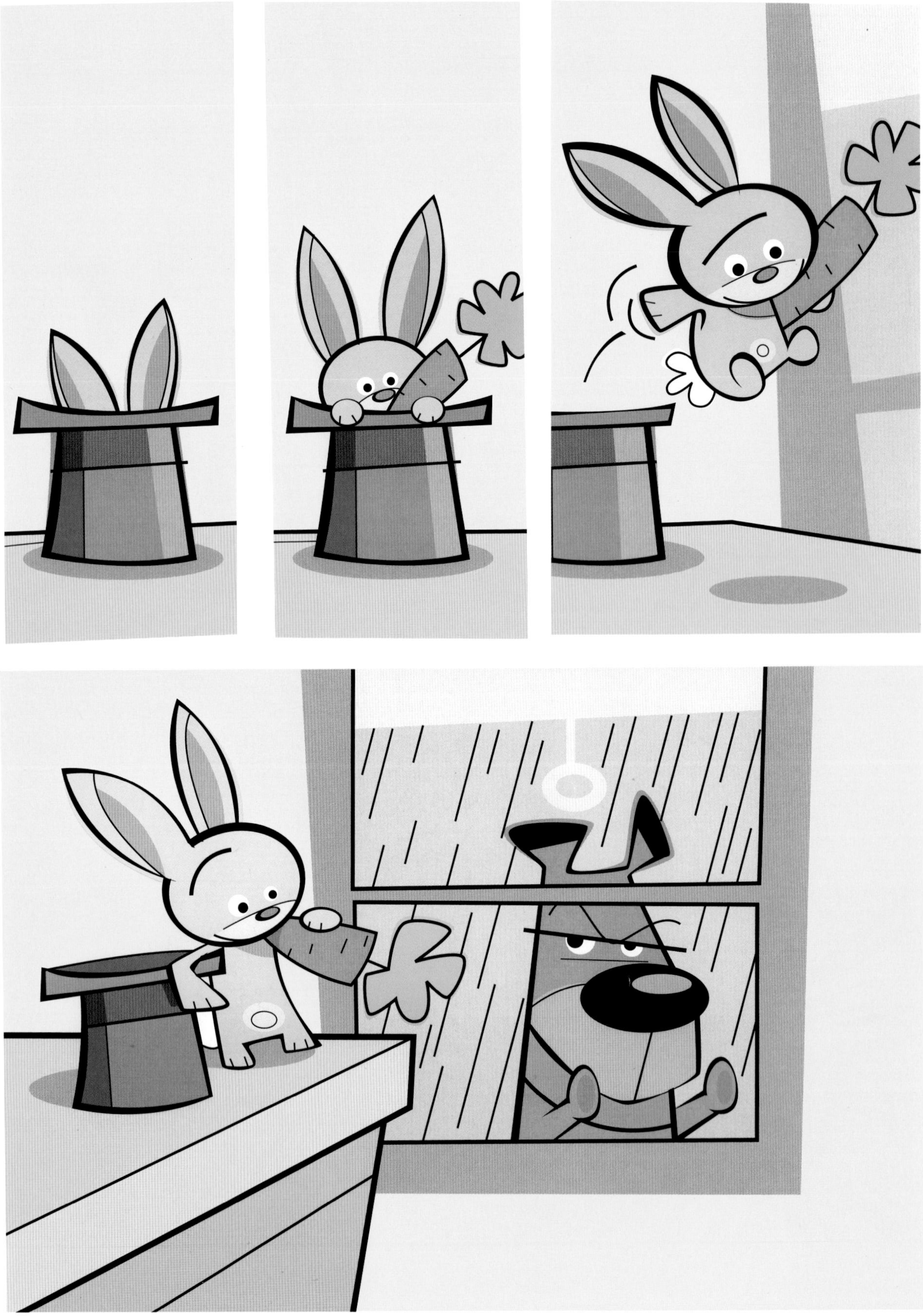